Elizabeth Gail and the Time for Love

Hilda Stahl

Tyndale House Publishers, Inc., Wheaton, Illinois

Dedicated with love to
Gerald and Marjory Cairns

The Elizabeth Gail Series

Cover and interior illustrations by Mort Rosenfeld

Library of Congress Catalog Card Number 88-51669
ISBN 0-8423-0813-X
Copyright 1983 by Hilda Stahl
All rights reserved
Printed in the United States of America

95   94   93   92   91   90
10   9   8   7   6   5   4   3   2

Contents

ONE
An unexpected guest

"Miss Johnson. Miss Johnson, I enjoyed your concert last night."

Elizabeth stepped into the cool shade of the building where Marv Secord had his office as she smiled at the girl who had spoken to her. Now that she was twenty-four she was getting used to being called Miss Johnson. "I'm glad you enjoyed the performance. It was quite a privilege to play at Grace Hall."

The girl took a deep breath and her dark eyes sparkled. "Someday I'm going to be a famous concert pianist just like you. I'm attending Maddox School of Music now. I know you were there a few years ago. I read all your reviews and attend all your concerts that I can."

"Thank you." Elizabeth smiled, then watched as the girl rushed down the almost deserted sidewalk toward the heart of the city. Being recognized and praised for her playing was as good as hearing the applause after a concert. She wanted to run after the girl and tell her never to let go of her dream, that it would come to pass if she was willing to work hard enough.

With a sigh Elizabeth pushed the strap of her purse up on her slender shoulder next to the ties of her yellow and white sundress. She touched her french braid which kept her long brown hair off her neck and back.

She pushed open the door and stepped into the air-conditioned office, her hazel eyes bright with excitement. "Good morning, Naomi. You look as if you're working too hard on such a beautiful Saturday."

The blonde woman looked up with a smile. "You look as if you're walking on air, Elizabeth. I was at the concert last night, so I know why you're so pleased with yourself. Mr. Secord said he's never heard you perform so magnificently!"

Elizabeth laughed gaily and just barely kept from spinning around the room. "Keep it up, Naomi. Those words are better than food."

"You're so enthusiastic, Elizabeth." Naomi glanced toward Marv's door and frowned. "Not like some people."

Elizabeth followed her look. "Who's in with Marv? I thought I was the only appointment he had this morning."

Naomi shrugged and her blue eyes were thoughtful. "Not everyone is as happy and bubbly as you are, Elizabeth." Naomi smiled. "I don't know how long Mr. Secord will be. Would you like a cup of coffee while you wait?"

Elizabeth shook her head. "I just had breakfast in my hotel room." She sat on a brown leather chair and crossed her slender legs, then set her purse on the carpeted floor beside her. "My parents are planning on us leaving for the farm just after twelve. Do you think Marv will need me longer?"

Naomi glanced at the door, then shook her head. "He'd tell me if he did. He knows you're going home for a vacation."

"I haven't been home with my family for more than a week at a time in years. I'm very thankful for this summer off. I know Marv wanted to keep me going, but I need time at home to rest and to practice on that baby grand I bought." She could picture the baby grand in the family room where Chuck had positioned it facing the fireplace. She knew Vera played it when she wasn't home, and she was glad.

Soon she'd be home again on the farm where she'd lived since she was eleven. The days of being an unloved foster child were in the long-ago past. The Johnsons had prayed her into their family, then adopted her. There were five children. Toby had been adopted also, but Ben, Susan, and Kevin were the real Johnsons. None of them were children now, though. She and Susan were the same age, and Susan had been married almost three years now. And so had Ben who was farming the Johnson farm as well as his own adjoining farm. Kevin was in his glory doing detective work and Toby had just signed a contract to teach history in the same high school they'd all attended. Would either Kevin or Toby get married this summer?

Naomi's phone buzzed and Elizabeth jumped. She heard Naomi say, "Yes, she's here. All right." She replaced the receiver. "Mr. Secord said to go right in, and he's sorry to have kept you waiting."

Elizabeth jumped up and grabbed her purse. She'd learn her fall schedule, then she'd meet Chuck and Vera and Tammy and head for home.

She reached to open the door but it swung in and

Marv greeted her, a tired look on his usually happy face as he ushered her into the small office.

She stopped dead, her heart rushing into her throat as Badden Lindsay stood up and turned to face her. Why hadn't Naomi told her the famous Badden Lindsay was here with Marv? She swallowed hard, suddenly feeling like a schoolgirl again as she remembered the first time she'd met him. She'd attended his concert at Grace Hall, then gone backstage afterward to shake his hand and tell him how wonderful his performance had been. She'd held out her hand, he'd taken it in his, and she'd forgotten his name and her comments and everything. She'd rushed out, her face flaming.

"Badden, you remember Elizabeth Johnson, don't you?" Marv sounded tense and Elizabeth shot him a look before she met Badden's dark eyes. His dark blond hair needed a trim and his lean face was almost as white as the shirt he wore with his dark brown slacks.

Badden's eyes narrowed and he shook his head. "I'm sorry, but no, I don't remember her. Is she a fan of mine?"

She stifled a gasp as color washed over her face. He didn't remember her! He didn't know that last night she'd played at Grace Hall just as he had every year for the past five years.

"She's a concert pianist, also, Badden," said Marv sharply as he tugged at his striped tie. He barely reached Elizabeth's shoulder and Badden's greater height dwarfed him even more. "I represent her also."

Badden barely inclined his head to Elizabeth as an apology, and she lifted her pointed chin higher, her hazel eyes challenging him. How could he not remember

10

her or recognize her name? She'd met him in Marv's office three years ago just before he'd left for Australia on a tour. And since then she'd made a name for herself in the business.

Suddenly Badden swayed and clutched at the back of the leather chair. Elizabeth reached to grab his arm but the look on his face made her drop her hands to her sides.

"Sit down again, Badden," snapped Marv, almost pushing the tall, thin man into the chair. He turned to Elizabeth. "Sit down so we can talk. I have a favor to ask."

Elizabeth frowned as she studied Marv's face. New lines ran from the corners of his eyes to his hairline. The lower part of his face was covered with a dark, well-trimmed beard and mustache. Finally she sank down on a chair next to Badden as Marv sat on his chair behind his large walnut desk. Morning light brightened the white phone on his desk. She swallowed the strange lump in her throat. "What's the favor, Marv?"

"Don't ask on my account," said Badden hoarsely. "My decision is final. Nothing this woman can do will make a difference to me."

"You never can tell." Marv leaned forward, his face earnest. "Elizabeth, Badden has been sick with the flu for over a week, and he can't shake it."

Elizabeth locked her fingers together in her lap. Her sundress suddenly felt very hot. Was Marv going to have her take Badden's tour? Could she fill the great man's shoes? He had been playing concert piano at least eight or ten years already.

Marv picked up a ballpoint pen, a gold one that Elizabeth had given him last year for Christmas, and fingered it nervously. "Badden has the strange notion that he wants to quit."

12

"Piano?" Elizabeth knew her voice was sharp with surprise and she snapped her mouth closed.

"Don't involve this girl with my problem," said Badden coldly. "It's none of her business what I do with my life."

Elizabeth wanted to turn on him and tell him just what she thought of giving up a dream, but Marv was talking.

"Badden, Elizabeth can be helpful if you'll just give me a chance to talk to her. You are too tired and worn out to think. You can't decide to quit when you're feeling this way."

"It's my life, Marv." Badden pushed himself up, then immediately dropped back down. "Get me to my hotel where I can get to bed, Marv."

"I will, Badden. Just be patient." Marv moved the picture of his wife and two children a fraction of an inch, then looked at Elizabeth. "You live on a farm. A quiet home away from noise and city life. Badden needs that now."

Badden gasped and Elizabeth just sat with her mouth open. She closed it and glanced at Badden who was staring at Marv, his face even whiter.

"No, Marv! It's out of the question," snapped Badden, gripping the arms of the leather chair until his knuckles were white.

Marv ignored Badden and kept his gray eyes on Elizabeth. "I want you to ask your parents if they can take Badden for the summer and put some life back into him."

Tiny shivers ran up and down her back and her stomach fluttered strangely.

"I won't go," said Badden harshly. "I am not a little

boy, Marv. I'm thirty years old and I've been on my own a long time."

"You have a contract with me, Badden, and I won't let you break it. Once you've had several weeks of rest, good country air, and home cooking, then you can decide about your future."

Badden sighed and leaned his head back, his eyes closed.

Elizabeth glanced at him and a warmth rushed through her. She must do what she could to keep this great musician from throwing away his career. "Marv, if you want the Johnson family to give Badden Lindsay a home for the summer, then consider it done. Our family will be honored."

Badden sat up straight and turned his head to stare at her. "You can't take in an absolute stranger."

"You aren't a stranger to me," she said evenly, her eyes meeting his without flinching.

"But your parents will surely object." He rubbed his jaw, then turned to glare at Marv. "How could you put me in this spot? How could you put . . . put . . . ." He searched for her name and Marv filled it in and Elizabeth suddenly seethed inside. How dare he forget who she was? "How could you put . . . Elizabeth . . . in this position? Her parents won't want me to interrupt their lives."

"Mr. Lindsay, my family is used to taking people in. They live that way. If someone needs a home for any reason, he can find a home with them. They will be glad to have you this summer. You'll find all the quiet and privacy you need." She turned back to Marv. "I'll call my parents and tell them."

Badden groaned.

Marv chuckled softly. "Thank you, Elizabeth. I knew you'd do this for Badden."

Badden's eyes flew open and he looked at Elizabeth as if he'd seen her for the first time. "Why should you do anything for me? We are strangers."

Elizabeth started to speak, but Marv said, "Elizabeth has been following your career from the first. She says that she wants to play the piano as well as the brilliant Badden Lindsay."

Elizabeth flushed painfully and wished she could fade out of sight. "There are thousands and thousands of people who want you to continue your career, Badden. It's unthinkable to give it up just because you feel out of it right now. A few weeks of rest will help you. My family will be glad to help you all they can."

"But they don't know me." Badden ran his fingers nervously through his hair. "I'll find a summer resort and go there on my own."

"No!" Marv pushed himself up. "No, Badden. You need looking after. You need Vera Johnson's home cooking to put a little meat on your bones. You need some normal activity around you with none of the pressures of a concert tour. You are going to the Johnson farm, and that's final!"

Badden sighed again. "I'm too tired and weak to fight anymore. I will go, but as soon as I'm on my feet again, I'm leaving."

"We'll talk about that later." Marv clamped his hand on Badden's bony shoulder. "You should've taken last summer off as I suggested. Now you are forced to take a vacation, but soon you'll be strong and healthy."

Elizabeth stood up and her sundress fell in graceful folds around her slender legs. "I'll make the arrangements for you to ride home with us today."

"I have my own car."

"That you can't drive!" Marv cut in sharply.

"I'll drive your car," said Elizabeth. "You can sleep all the way to the farm."

Badden stood up and even though Elizabeth was tall for a girl, he was taller. "I'll be packed and ready whenever you say." He sounded as if he'd rather be going to jail. "I'll call a taxi so I can get back to my hotel."

"I'll drive you if you'll wait a minute in my outer office," said Marv as he walked to the door and held it open. "I need a few minutes alone with Elizabeth."

Badden walked out slowly, his shoulders stooped so that he looked much older than his thirty years.

Elizabeth walked to the window and looked out, then turned as Marv closed the door. "Do you think it's wise to force him to go to the farm?"

Marv nodded and rubbed his beard. "He needs the time, Elizabeth. And he needs to be around a Christian family. He has lost hope. He needs love. He needs to know of God's love for him. Your family is the answer to my prayer for Badden."

Elizabeth moistened her lips with the tip of her tongue. She suddenly realized that the famous Badden Lindsay would be on the farm all summer. And she would, too.

She turned away to hide a smile.

TWO
Home on the farm

Elizabeth glanced at her watch and realized in surprise that she'd been driving Badden's silver Mercedes for two hours already. As she looked at the station wagon ahead of her on the expressway, she could see Chuck and Vera in the front seat with Tammy LaDere in the back. And behind Tammy and on the luggage rack on top of the station wagon was Elizabeth's and Tammy's luggage with a few things of Badden's that wouldn't fit in the trunk of the Mercedes.

"Are you sure you still want me to come for the summer, Libby?" Tammy had whispered when she'd learned that Badden was spending the summer on the farm. "It might be too much for your family."

Elizabeth had shaken her head. Three years ago when she'd learned that Tammy LaDere was not just her look-alike cousin, but her half sister, she'd claimed her as family and so had the Johnsons. At times it was still hard to believe that Frank Dobbs had been the father of both Tammy and herself. "You are coming, Tammy. We won't give up our chance to go to Sandhill Ranch this year. We've been trying to go for three years now. This time we're going to make it!"

So Tammy had given in, but had insisted on riding with Chuck and Vera. "You said Badden needs his rest, Libby. If I rode with you we'd be talking the entire time. Badden would not find that restful."

Elizabeth had had to agree. She glanced at him and found him looking at her with his brows raised. "What?" she asked, forcing a smile. He hadn't said anything since he'd met her parents and Tammy.

"I can't believe strangers would take me in and treat me as if they'd always known me. What's the catch?"

She gasped, her eyes wide. "Catch! There's no catch. We care about people. Is that hard to understand?"

"No one does something for nothing."

"Oh, no? Then you will find that you're wrong. Chuck and Vera Johnson are givers! They give their time and their love freely to others. They've always been that way. But I suppose you'll have to learn that yourself." She couldn't believe he could be so distrustful, so bitter against people. When he walked out on a stage to play, he radiated a magnetism, even a love and a caring. Why didn't any of that show now? Was it because he was very weak? Or had she only imagined it during the performance because she'd had him on a pedestal all these years?

"I'm sure you only see what they want you to see."

She forced back anger as she gripped the steering wheel tighter. "I've lived with them for thirteen years now, and I think that I know them very well."

"Are you adopted?" he asked in surprise.

"Yes." She wouldn't go into detail about how her real mother had beaten her and starved her and locked her

18

in a closet, or how she'd gone from one bad foster home to another, then back to Mother to be mistreated again, then to other foster homes. By the time she was taken in by the Johnsons, she'd known all about life—at least the bad side.

Badden reached across and slipped a cassette into the player and the car filled with a piano concerto.

He didn't speak again until he stepped out of the car at the Johnson farm and Goosy Poosy ran toward him with his long white neck out, his wings spread, honking wildly.

"What's that?" He pressed against the car and Elizabeth ran around with a laugh as she shooed the goose away.

"He's not only a watchdog, but he's also a pet," she said, keeping herself between Badden and Goosy Poosy.

"Welcome to our home, Badden," said Chuck with a warm smile as he and Vera walked from the back of the station wagon toward the Mercedes. "I see Alan forgot to lock Goosy Poosy in the chicken pen."

"He took me by surprise," said Badden with a slight smile.

"The first day Elizabeth came here, he flew against her and knocked her down," said Vera, laughing. "We've tried to keep that from happening again."

Elizabeth wrinkled her nose. "It took me a long time to get over my fear of Goosy Poosy."

"Let's go in out of the hot sun," said Chuck as he lifted luggage out of the station wagon. He stopped and frowned thoughtfully. "I wonder why Peggy and Alan aren't out here. They usually burst out of the house when we drive in." He stood with his hands lightly on his hips as he looked around. He was dressed in tan slacks with a short-sleeved white dress shirt opened at the neck. A slight breeze ruffled his graying red hair.

"Maybe they didn't hear us," said Vera as she tugged her knit top over her light blue dress pants. The sun made her blonde hair almost silver.

Just then they heard a shout from the field in back of the cow barn and Elizabeth shielded her eyes to see who had shouted.

Suddenly two calves ran into the yard with Alan and Peggy behind them. Elizabeth dropped her purse next to the car and dashed out to head off the calves before they could run down the long drive onto the road. Chuck shouted and blocked the way between the house and the chicken coop.

Elizabeth twisted her ankle, then caught herself on the person closest to her. She looked up to find Badden beside her, his face flushed and damp with perspiration. The great Badden Lindsay had helped round up the calves! Her stomach fluttered and she quickly dropped her hand.

"Did you hurt yourself?" he asked in concern.

She shook her head, suddenly unable to speak. She stood beside him in the driveway and watched Chuck and Alan close the large wooden gate after the calves. Peggy and Tammy leaned on the fence, gasping for air, and Vera stood beside the picnic table near the back door, her hair disheveled, her face red.

"I think I'd better sit down," said Badden in a strange voice and Elizabeth looked at him quickly. He was white around his lips and looked ready to collapse.

"You shouldn't have helped with the calves," she said as she took his arm and walked him to his car.

"I've wanted to do that since I watched Westerns on

TV." He sank down in the passenger seat and leaned his elbows on his bony knees and his face in his hands.

Helplessly Elizabeth stood looking down on him. Finally he looked up and grinned weakly.

"I wasn't as strong as I thought, but I'm all right now. Don't look so scared. I'm not going to drop dead at your feet."

"Of course you're not!" She picked up her purse and pushed a stray strand of hair that had escaped from the french braid behind her ear. "I'll show you to your room so you can rest before supper." She turned just as Peggy called her name, then flung her arms around her.

"I'm glad you're home, Elizabeth! I couldn't wait to see you again! How was your concert last night?" Peggy's brown eyes glowed and her brown hair bounced around her slender shoulders. Before Elizabeth could speak Peggy turned and flung her arms around Badden. "I'm glad to meet you! You must be Elizabeth's boyfriend. I told her she'd fall in love one of these days and get married."

Elizabeth flushed and Badden looked astonished. "Peggy," said Elizabeth when she could find her voice. "This is Badden Lindsay. He's our guest for the summer. Badden, this is Peggy Greentree."

Peggy flipped her hair back and grinned. "You're too old to be a foster kid like Alan and me. But I'm glad to meet you. Can you ride? Or swim?"

He opened his mouth to speak, then closed it as he looked helplessly at Elizabeth.

"Peggy, you can get acquainted with Badden later. I'm going to take him in and show him his room. I'll talk to you later."

Peggy immediately turned to Tammy and started

talking with her while Alan and Chuck unloaded the luggage.

Elizabeth and Badden stopped beside Vera. "Mom, does Badden go in the guest room?"

Vera nodded. "And Tammy will share with you."

"I think you have a houseful already, Vera," said Badden. "I could go to a motel."

"You are staying with us!"

"That's right!" Elizabeth gripped his arm and walked him to the back door. "Do I have to use force?"

He flushed, then she laughed.

"I'm only teasing, Badden. I only want you to get some rest so you can cope with all of us."

"I'm not used to dealing with a large family."

"You probably feel more at home at a piano."

He stopped at the bottom of the stairs and looked at her. "Yes, I do. A piano asks nothing in return."

She frowned. "Badden, we will ask nothing of you."

He looked deep into her eyes and her heart seemed to stop. "I hope not, Elizabeth, for I have nothing to give."

Abruptly she turned and started up the stairs. "I'll ask Alan to bring your luggage up so that you can rest." At the first door on her right she said, "This is Alan's room. Across is Mom and Dad's. This is Kevin's, then Toby's. Across is Peggy's and mine. And you'll have this room." She pushed open the door. "The bathroom is at the end of the hall."

He walked in and went straight to the bed where he sank down wearily. "Tell Alan not to bother with my things. I'll bring them up after I rest awhile."

Elizabeth shook her head as she lowered the blinds to block out the bright sun. "Alan will bring up your luggage and you can unpack at your leisure. Would you like something to eat or drink before you sleep?" For some reason she didn't want to leave him.

He shook his head and finally she turned to leave. Before she closed the door he said, "Elizabeth."

She stopped, then looked at him again.

"Thank you for driving me here, and for your hospitality. I do appreciate you and your family."

"You're welcome," she whispered, then closed the door quickly, her hand trembling. What was wrong with her? She had been around famous people often in the past few years and she'd never felt this way before.

Finally she took a deep breath, lifted her chin, and walked back downstairs. She met Chuck and Alan at the bottom.

"Is Badden all settled in?" asked Chuck.

"Yes. But you can take his stuff in to him. I told him you would." She grinned at Alan who was struggling with two heavy cases. "Do you need a little help?"

"I can handle these. I might be short, but I'm strong." He grinned and his blue eyes twinkled. "Someday I'll be as tall as your boyfriend."

"He is not my boyfriend!" She glanced quickly up the stairs and lowered her voice. "Don't you dare tease him, Alan. He's not used to being teased."

"Who was teasing? All I've heard since I moved here was Badden this and Badden that."

"Alan," said Chuck in a warning voice. "Elizabeth has a high regard for Badden's talent. That doesn't mean she's in love with him."

"Nor ever will be!" she cried, then turned at a sound. Badden stood at the top of the stairs and she knew by his face that he'd heard the conversation. She wanted to vanish in a puff of smoke, but instead she turned and walked away, her back stiff and her head high.

She stopped just outside the back door and sagged against the house, her shoulder almost touching the small bell hanging there.

"Is the excitement of being home too much for you?" asked Tammy with a laugh as she set down the suitcase she'd been carrying.

Elizabeth looked at her and it was as if she were looking in a mirror except Tammy had blue eyes and she was not as thin as Elizabeth. "I just made such a fool of myself." She told Tammy what had happened and her face flamed. "I am so embarrassed!"

"Forget it even happened. Badden won't think anything about it. He will know that boys like to tease, and he'll only think you were trying to keep Alan from teasing you further."

"But he looked so stricken! And I don't know why. He doesn't want anyone to get personally involved with him. But it would hurt your pride, I guess, to hear someone say that she'd never fall in love with you." Elizabeth groaned and wrapped her arms across herself.

Tammy sighed, then picked up the suitcase. "All right. Take this up to Badden and tell him that you'll be happy to fall in love with him."

Elizabeth gasped and shook her head. "I'll take it to him, but I won't say a word."

Tammy chuckled. "You'd better not even take it to him. It's mine."

Elizabeth looked at Tammy, then laughed, feeling better. "All right. I'm overreacting. I just want the man to recover so that he won't consider leaving the business. I can't imagine him not playing concert piano!

It would be as if I'd quit! And I would never do that. Never!"

Before Tammy could speak again, the back door opened and Chuck and Alan walked out for more luggage. Alan winked at Elizabeth as Chuck said, "I explained to Badden about Alan's teasing. He seemed to understand."

Elizabeth nodded as she forced back a flush.

"Where's your boyfriend, Elizabeth?" called Peggy from the back of the station wagon and Alan burst out laughing.

"I give up," said Elizabeth between her teeth. "I'm going to my room and rest!"

Tammy caught her arm. "Don't be so touchy or they'll continue to tease you."

Elizabeth finally nodded. "I guess you're right." Why was she so touchy? Why was she making such a big deal out of it?

She walked to the station wagon and lifted out a bag of piano books. "When will you play your guitar for me, Peggy?"

Peggy's face lit up and her eyes lost the mischievous twinkle. "As soon as we're done unloading. I've learned a lot since you were home last."

"Let's go swimming first," said Alan from beside Elizabeth. "You haven't had much time to swim in the pool since Dad had it built last summer."

Elizabeth felt very hot and sticky all of a sudden. "I would like to go swimming. And then, Peggy, I want to hear you play."

"Maybe Badden wants to swim, too," said Peggy.

"I already asked him," said Alan. "He said he's going to take a nap."

Several minutes later Elizabeth stood on the diving board poised for a dive while the others splashed in the water below. She hesitated, then glanced at the guest room window. Her heart stopped. Badden was watching her and she flushed and quickly dove in, the water closing in over her head. But the sight of him all alone and looking very lonely stayed with her.

Peggy splashed her and Alan dunked her and she laughed with her head back, water dripping down her. Tammy raced across the pool with her and Tammy beat her. Finally she pulled herself up on the edge of the pool and sat gasping for breath. Next to the others' suntans she felt ghostly white. Her dark red one-piece suit would have looked better on Tammy.

Elizabeth squirmed, determined not to lift her eyes to the second floor guest room window. But she looked and her eyes locked with Badden's and she felt as if she were back in the water again with it closing forever over her head.

He turned away and she fought against the pain she felt. He was locked inside himself, and she didn't know how to set him free.

THREE
A talk with Badden

Elizabeth finished the Chopin sonata, feeling tired but exhilarated after three hours of playing. The tone and the touch of the baby grand were fantastic, and she turned with a pleased smile. The smile faded as she stared at Badden Lindsay sitting on a chair out of her line of vision. "When did you come in?" she asked barely above a whisper.

He leaned back and stretched out his long legs. "You have such heart when you play, Elizabeth!" The words seemed to spring from him against his will.

"Thank you." She sat on the edge of the bench, dressed in yellow shorts and a suntop with her hair pulled back and tied with a yellow ribbon at the nape of her slender neck.

"I am sorry that I never heard you perform." His eyes were dark, his face intense. "You have a gift. Never, never let it go!"

"I won't. But Badden, you have a gift, too. I have heard you play. I have sat in the audience and felt captivated by you. You cannot, dare not quit! The world could not, I could not survive without you!"

He shot from the chair and stood over her, his fists clenched at his sides. "What do you know about surviving? *I* must survive! *I* must learn to live! Do you know that my entire life has been spent at the piano? I could not join in the swimming because I can't swim! Do you know how much of a freak I am? I play the piano and that is all I do!"

She eased herself up and she stood so close to him that she almost touched him. She could feel his ragged breathing on her face and smell his after-shave lotion. "Badden, I will teach you to swim. I will teach you anything you want to learn."

He gripped her arms and hauled her against him, then kissed her savagely until her lungs ached for air and her head spun. Why wasn't she outraged? Why didn't she struggle?

She closed her eyes and clutched the front of his shirt. When he lifted his head she stayed against him, her breathing ragged, her knees weak.

"You should hate me," he said hoarsely. "You should slap my face."

"I could never do that," she whispered, her hazel eyes wide.

His arms tightened and he kissed her again, this time tenderly. Abruptly he released her and strode across to the empty fireplace and she felt as if a part of her were missing. He turned to face her and she saw a muscle jump in his jaw. "Forgive me, Elizabeth. I shouldn't have kissed you."

She tried to speak. No one had kissed her since she'd broken up with Jerry Grosbeck five years ago. Finally she said, "There is nothing to forgive." Her voice cracked and she could feel her cheeks burning.

"You are very vulnerable right now, Elizabeth. You are ready to fall in love and since you see me in need, you could easily fall for me."

She gasped and dropped down on the piano bench, her eyes on Badden.

"I know that you are a very loving, passionate woman. I can tell by your playing. Please don't waste your feelings on me. I am empty inside. I have no feelings, no love to give. And you would need love in return."

She burned with embarrassment. Did he think that she loved him? She forced life into her legs and she pushed herself up, her chin high. "Badden, I'm sorry if you think that I'm a love-starved woman who would fall for the first attractive man who kisses me. Put your mind at rest. I have a career to think about. This is not the time for love for me! Maybe in another ten years or so." She stepped toward him. Could he tell she was trembling? "You have nothing to fear from me, Badden. I will teach you to swim and to ride a horse and to milk a cow if you want. I will be your friend just as the others are in this family. Can I say it any plainer?"

He stabbed his fingers through his dark blond hair. "I can agree to you teaching me. Thank you." He pushed his hands into his pants pockets. "If you find yourself falling in love with me, please tell me so that I can leave here."

She gasped. How dare he! "You are very egotistical, Badden Lindsay! Do I look that starved for love?"

"I didn't mean to make you angry." He stepped toward her, but she stepped back, bumping into the piano.

"Do you think you can casually tell a girl not to fall in

love with you without making her angry?"

"I have not had a girl close to me to tell it to."

"And you still don't!"

Something flickered in his eyes and she thought for a minute it was pain, but then it was gone. "Then we understand each other."

"I understand you completely. You want to stay behind that wall you've built up. You don't want to tear it down yourself, and you certainly won't allow anyone else to tear it down." She rubbed her damp palms down her shorts and her chest rose and fell. "You are afraid to be a man with a man's feelings. You say you want to live, but you can't live with that wall around you!"

His face was so white she thought he was going to faint. "If the wall comes down, then I will surely die," he said barely above a whisper in a voice full of agony.

She moistened her lips with the tip of her tongue. "Why, Badden?"

He shook his head. "I cannot say!"

"You mean you won't say! You won't trust me, will you? You're so afraid that I might step over the boundaries you've laid for me, that you won't trust me. You must trust someone sometime."

He squared his broad shoulders. "I have lived this long without trusting anyone. I can continue this way."

"Oh, Badden." Tears stung her eyes and she blinked rapidly.

"Don't waste tears on me, Elizabeth. I'm not worth it!"

"Yes! Yes, you are! You are a gifted man! You have more than most to offer." She brushed her hand across her eyes. "God made you, Badden. He gave you the gift of music."

Badden shook his head with a scowl, and tapped his

chest with his fist. "*I* gave myself the gift of music! Or maybe my mother did. She made me practice hour after hour when other boys were playing outdoors. She made me practice when I hated it. When I knew that was all I could ever do well, I made myself sit for hours, playing."

Elizabeth walked around an overstuffed chair and stood behind it, her hands clutching the coarse tweed. "Don't let the past cloud the future, Badden. What's done is done. Look ahead. You have a brilliant future! Learn about God. He loves you. He wants to make your life abundantly successful and happy."

"I can't understand, Elizabeth."

And she knew he couldn't, because the Bible said that Satan had blinded the eyes of the unbeliever so that he couldn't see spiritual truth. Silently she prayed for the eyes of his understanding to be opened. Before the summer was over she wanted him to see that God loved him and wanted to be his strength and help.

She smiled. "Badden, let's leave this for now. How would you like to go swimming?"

He hesitated. "I have nothing to wear."

"You met my brother Ben last night. You're close to his size, so we'll borrow swim trunks from him."

Still he hesitated. He locked his long fingers behind his back. "I will look foolish."

"I won't laugh."

"The others will."

He suddenly looked very young and boyish and she knew his pride would suffer if anyone did tease or laugh. "We'll only go in if the others aren't around."

He studied her thoughtfully, then nodded. "But why do you bother with me?"

She spread out her hands, palms up. "I really don't know!" Then she laughed. "Don't swing from side to side, Badden. First you're egotistical and then you're humble. Which is it to be?"

His face darkened with anger. "Are you making fun of me?"

"Oh, no! I was teasing you, and that's different from making fun. I didn't mean to hurt your feelings."

He stiffened. "I think I'll go to my room and read. Forget about swimming."

"No way! You said you'd go, and I'm keeping you to your word." She laughed up at him and took his arm. She felt him stiffen, then he relaxed and grinned. "We'll go see Ben and Jill. And we'll get trunks for you to wear."

He shook his head. "What am I getting myself into?"

"You'll see, Badden Lindsay. And if you relax, you just might enjoy yourself." She led him out the front door. "I am going to give you a little of your childhood right now when you're thirty."

He stopped beside the maple where the swing hung from a fat branch. "How much of your childhood did you spend on this swing?"

She grabbed the rope and sat down on the board. "Not enough. Give me a push, will you?"

He pushed her a little on the back. He caught the swing and walked forward, pushing higher and higher, then he released it as he stepped aside and she squealed with delight. She flashed past him and saw that he was smiling and her heart leaped.

When she stopped she jumped out and caught the ropes again. "You get in, Badden, and I'll push you."

He hesitated, then sat down and held the ropes, his bony elbows poking the air.

She tried to push him as high as he had her, but she didn't have the strength. "Pump a little," she called. "Lean forward when you're out there, then lean back when you come back here. Keep your feet and legs out straight!"

She pushed him again and again, laughing with delight. Finally his laughter floated around her and it was the most beautiful sound she'd ever heard. He coasted until his swinging slowed, then stopped himself by dropping his feet to the ground where the grass was rubbed bare from many other feet.

Cricket barked and ran to them as they walked down the long drive. He wagged his stubby tail and his curvy back end wagged, too.

Elizabeth knelt beside the cocker spaniel and playfully tugged the long golden ears. "You stay home, Cricket. You can't go with us."

"I suppose he understands every word you say."

She looked up at Badden with a grin. "Of course." She ordered Cricket to the house, then stood with Badden until Cricket disappeared around the end of the garage. "We used to have a dog named Rex. He was beautiful and he loved me best. He always understood what I said."

"What happened to him?"

She looked off across the road to the tree-covered land. "He just got too old to live. Did you know that geese live longer than dogs?"

He shook his head. The sun brightened his hair to a lighter blonde. "Is that important to know?"

"It is to Goosy Poosy. Some geese live to be thirty years old."

"Hey, don't make it sound so old."

"You're still young, Badden. You have plenty of time to learn all the things you want to learn." She walked beside him down the road to the small house where Ben and Jill lived.

"Your sister-in-law looks as if she's going to have that baby any day now."

Elizabeth nodded. "In July. She and I were best friends in school. I told you she's a writer. She's had a children's book published."

"I'm impressed. Your brother farms and his wife writes. That's quite a combination."

She turned and pointed down the road the other way. "Jill's parents live in that house. Not the first one, but the second one that you can barely see. Her mother won't have far to go to help her when the baby arrives."

"Are your parents looking forward to being grandparents?"

A ground squirrel zipped across the road and Elizabeth jumped, then laughed. "They have a granddaughter already. Susan and Jerry have a year-old daughter. You'll meet them tonight. Susan and I are the same age."

"And do you wish that you were married with a baby?" Badden stopped and she did, too. He watched her closely.

"I am happy to be a concert pianist. That is my dream." She started to walk again and he fell into step beside her. "When I first came here I had two dreams. One was to be adopted by the Johnson family and the other was to be a concert pianist." She looked up at him and her eyes misted over. "Both dreams have come true."

"That's wonderful."

She kicked a clump of grass off the road into the ditch. "What was your dream, Badden?"

He didn't answer and she looked at him to find a thoughtful expression on his thin face. "I guess to be happy."

"And what will make you happy?" she asked in a quiet voice.

"I don't know."

"I know."

"What?"

"God has created a God-shaped vacuum in each person's life, in your life, Badden. Until you fill that empty space with God, nothing will satisfy you."

"No one has ever told me that before. I can tell that you're not just talking about religion."

Elizabeth stopped in Ben's short drive with a shake of her head. The yellow ribbon came loose and her hair cascaded around her slender shoulders and down her back. Badden picked up the ribbon, looked at it, and stuffed it into his pocket.

"Not religion, but a personal relationship with God, your Creator. A close relationship in which God is your heavenly Father and Jesus is your brother."

Before she could say anything else Jill stepped outside and called to them.

"We came to borrow swim trunks for Badden," said Elizabeth as they walked to the door. "Is that possible, Jill?"

She grinned and stepped aside for them to enter. "I'll get the dark blue nylon ones." She sighed and looked down at herself. "I will be glad when our baby is out here instead of inside. And then I can enjoy swimming again."

Elizabeth laughed, then looked at Badden's red face. How long would it take for him to be used to all of them? With God and the Johnson family working together, Badden was going to be a new man by the end of the summer. She would help him find the happiness that he desired. And she wouldn't fall in love with him either!

FOUR
Sandhill Ranch

Elizabeth followed Tammy out of the small plane onto
the airstrip at Belmont, Nebraska, the small town
closest to Sandhill Ranch. Hot wind whipped her hair
across her face, and pressed her burnt orange dress
pants and white knit shirt into her slender frame. She
held her hair back with one hand and clutched her
purse and travel case with the other. She watched
Tammy struggle to keep her skirt down, her hair out of
her face, and her purse from falling off her shoulder.

Elizabeth almost stumbled through the door of the
small building where Mark McCall had told them to
wait until someone picked them up. She stood just
inside the door, thankful for the air conditioning and
the protection from the wind. Her skin felt gritty and
she remembered the other trips to Nebraska with the
blowing sand and hot wind.

"Is it always like this?" asked Tammy breathlessly as
she tried to push her hair into some order. "We must
find a restroom before anyone sees us like this." She

rolled her eyes at Elizabeth. "Your rancher will run away and hide if he sees us now."

"My rancher?" Elizabeth laughed as she walked with Tammy around a few chairs to the ladies' room.

"Nolen Brown." Tammy dropped her purse and gave a little shriek as she looked in the large mirror over the sink. "Is that really me?"

"Now, Tammy, it isn't that bad. Maybe we should braid our hair so that the wind can't tangle it. And if you had on pants instead of a dress you wouldn't have to work so hard to keep together."

Tammy brushed vigorously at her long brown hair. "I should've listened to you, but I couldn't imagine any of this. I didn't think you really meant a small plane would have to take us from Omaha to O'Neill and then another small plane from there to here. I didn't know it would be so hot and so windy! Oh, I can't show my face!"

Elizabeth slowly brushed her hair, glancing at Tammy from time to time. She had never seen Tammy so tense or so determined to look just right. Finally Elizabeth dropped her brush into her purse and turned to Tammy. "Relax and you'll enjoy yourself a whole lot more."

Tammy stood with her brush clasped tightly in her hand, her blue eyes wide. "I feel so . . . so . . . I don't know! I've never been here before. My own dad lived here. Our dad. He walked through this small town and he lived on the ranch we're going to, and he left part of that ranch to you. And you're sharing it with me." Her eyes grew rounder. "I can't relax! I feel as if my entire life will be changed because of this visit. I'll never be the same again. Don't you feel it?"

Elizabeth shook her head. "But I guess I can understand a little of what you're saying. Still, relax and enjoy it." She picked up her case along with her purse. "We'd better get out there so that Mark or Nolen will know we're here."

The small plane had already taken off, and an attendant had set the heavy luggage near a wall for Elizabeth and Tammy. Elizabeth sat on a chair near the luggage but Tammy said she couldn't settle down enough to sit still. She walked to the large window overlooking the landing strip and Elizabeth crossed her long legs and sat back, trying to get comfortable in the molded plastic folding chair.

"What is so important in Nebraska that you must go now?" Badden had asked her last night while they sat side by side on the edge of the swimming pool. After two weeks he was an adequate swimmer.

"Tammy and I have been planning this trip for three years. We must go." She had looked at him and realized that she would miss him. "Toby promised to teach you lifesaving, and he'll go riding with you every day." She had stopped and really looked at him. "You are getting quite brown and your hair is a lighter blond. No one will recognize you when you go on tour this fall."

"And am I going on tour, Elizabeth?"

She frowned impatiently. "Of course you are. You have your health back, and by the end of summer you'll have so much energy you'll want to give two concerts a day."

"I might decide to stay here. Ben said that he could use me here on the farm if I decide I want to stay."

"I won't listen to that kind of talk!" She toppled him into the water and fell in beside him. He bobbed up and swung the water from his face and caught her to him, his body hard against hers.

"Don't go to Nebraska," he'd said in a low, fierce voice.

She knew he had felt her heart thudding against him. "I must," she had managed to whisper.

"Don't let one of those cowboys rope you and tie you to him."

She had forced a laugh and struggled until he finally released her. "I'll be back in three weeks without a cowboy. I wouldn't mess up my career by falling in love."

"See that you don't!" He had pushed himself out of the pool, grabbed his towel and walked to the house.

This morning he had not gotten up to say good-bye and Chuck had taken Elizabeth and Tammy to the airport.

She sighed and moved restlessly in her chair. Three weeks seemed an eternity.

"Libby!"

She jumped up at Nolen's call, then gasped as she watched Nolen grab Tammy in a tight hug. And to Elizabeth's surprise Tammy returned the hug. Nolen looked at her a minute, then kissed her.

Elizabeth grinned. What would Nolen say when he realized he was kissing Tammy so lovingly instead of Elizabeth Johnson?

Tammy stepped back and her blue eyes sparkled and her cheeks flushed rosy red. "That's the kind of welcome I like!"

Nolen chuckled and then looked at Elizabeth. "Hi, Libby. I just gave your hug and kiss to your sister."

Elizabeth laughed at the look on Tammy's face. "And when did you realize it wasn't me?"

He pushed his broad-brimmed hat to the back of his head and his eyes crinkled as he laughed. He winked at Tammy. "I knew it just as I reached to hug her, and then I couldn't help myself. I fell head over heels in love."

"Sure you did," said Tammy, blushing hotly. "What other tall tales are we in for?"

"When you put Mark and Nolen together, you get all the tall stories you can handle," said Elizabeth with a grin at Nolen. She liked his jeans and Western shirt. His brown boots were shiny and new looking.

"Let's get you loaded. I hope you don't mind the pickup. That mower broke down again and I had to bring the part in today. We tried hard to be done haying before you got here, but we didn't quite make it." He picked up two large cases and they followed him, each carrying the small cases.

Tammy nudged Elizabeth, then leaned close and whispered, "Let me sit beside Nolen, please."

Elizabeth raised her eyebrows and grinned, but Tammy shrugged and said please again.

The wind whipped her hair across her face and Elizabeth wished that she'd taken the time to braid it. She saw Tammy struggling to keep her skirt down again. Nolen whistled a loud, long wolf whistle and Tammy blushed a brighter red.

Inside the pickup Elizabeth leaned against the door, glad to be out of the hot wind. Perspiration dotted her face and she wanted to be home again in the pool with Badden.

Nolen climbed in and slammed the door. "We'll soon have it cool in here. Air conditioning is a marvelous invention." He started the pickup and turned on the air and Elizabeth sighed in relief. "One minute you're so hot you think you're going to melt right into your boots, then you cool right down and you're ready to live again." He tipped his hat back again and looked at Tammy. "We can go right home, or we can stop for a bite to eat."

"I'm not hungry," said Tammy in a voice that didn't sound like hers.

"I could use a tall glass of something cold," said Elizabeth. "But I don't mind drinking it as we drive if you have to hurry back with that mower part."

Nolen was able to take his eyes off Tammy long enough to wink at Elizabeth. "We'll stop at the Dairy Queen and have a slush. Does that suit you?"

She nodded and Tammy said it did sound good.

At the Dairy Queen Nolen hopped out and ran inside and Tammy turned to Elizabeth. "Do you think he's serious? Did he fall for me?"

Elizabeth squeezed Tammy's hand. "I don't want you to feel bad, but I think that's his way of joking."

She groaned and covered her face. Finally she looked up. "I don't want him to be joking. The minute he touched me, I fell in love."

"No!" Elizabeth shook her head in shock. "You can't mean it! You don't even know the man."

"I know how I feel. I know that I want to get acquainted with him. I want to know everything about him. I love him. I can't believe this is happening to me!" Tammy locked her hands over her purse, a tragic look on her face.

"Here he comes. Smile, Tammy."

She opened the door for him and he handed them tall containers of orange slush, then climbed in with his own.

He smiled at Tammy. "Did you miss me?"

"Yes."

"I missed you like crazy."

Elizabeth sipped her drink through the straw and felt sick inside. Nolen had no idea what he was doing to Tammy. Or did he mean every word he said?

42

As Nolen drove fast down the highway, Elizabeth watched the rolling countryside, dotted with cattle and occasional windmills. There were grassy hillsides and blue sky as far as the eye could see.

Finally Nolen slowed and turned onto a dirt road that Elizabeth knew led to the ranch. Wouldn't Badden love this? Maybe someday she could bring Badden here. She frowned and pushed thoughts of Badden away. She would think about her Nebraska friends.

"You're in for a surprise, Libby," said Nolen as he pulled into the sandy drive of Sandhill Ranch.

Elizabeth watched expectantly as he drove past the house where the McCall family lived to a small house shaded by a large cottonwood. The house hadn't been there before.

"You and Tammy can have this place to yourselves while you're here," said Nolen as he opened the door. Sand blew in and swirled around his feet.

"But we can stay in the other house," she said. "We don't want to make someone leave here."

Nolen chuckled and shook his head. "This is my place and I'm staying with the McCalls so that you two girls can have all the privacy you want. I even have a piano."

Elizabeth opened her door and jumped out, looking around excitedly. "We're going to have a great vacation, Tammy."

Tammy nodded and walked toward the small house. "It reminds me of Ben and Jill's home."

"It's air-conditioned," said Nolen as he pushed open the door and stepped aside for them to enter. He dropped the luggage, then pushed the door closed. "What do you think?"

"I love it!" cried Tammy as she turned in a slow circle.

"It is wonderful!" Elizabeth touched the upright piano and looked around the room that was a kitchen, dining, and living room combined.

"The bathroom's through that door and the other two doors lead into bedrooms." Nolen pushed open a door. "Tammy, you take this one and Libby the other."

"I hate to make you give up your house," said Tammy, hesitating in the doorway.

"I'm bunking with Mark. He doesn't snore too loud."

Elizabeth set her purse on the chair next to her bed and pushed her hair out of her face. The room was small but very clean. It had a double bed, a chair and a dresser along with a small closet. She wanted to drop down on the bed and go to sleep. Last night she'd lain awake a long time, trying to figure out why Badden had asked her not to go to Nebraska. Finally she'd drifted off to sleep only to dream about him. And once again he was kissing her and she was kissing him.

She flushed and touched her lips gingerly. She wouldn't think about that silly dream!

She walked to the door, then stopped in the open doorway. Nolen and Tammy stood beside the couch just looking at each other. Elizabeth's heart skipped a beat. Would a man ever look at her the way Nolen was looking at Tammy?

FIVE
Love problems

Elizabeth reined in Sweet Water at the top of the hill and waited for Tammy. Oh, but the sky looked big and blue today! She watched Tammy rein in Peaches, a golden palomino. "Tammy, look around! You can see for miles. Isn't that an incredible sight?"

Tammy breathed deeply, then flipped a long braid over her slender shoulder. She looked at home in the saddle with her Western shirt and jeans. "I love the sandhills! For the first time in my life I feel as if I belong, really belong. Do you know what I mean?"

Elizabeth moved and the saddle creaked. She rubbed her hand down her jeans and swallowed hard. "Tammy, we've been here almost a week and I've been trying to have a serious talk with you."

Peaches swished a fly away with her long white tail as Tammy sighed. "Is that why you were so determined that we come alone this morning?"

Elizabeth nodded. "I've been watching you and Nolen and it worries me. Does he know you're serious and not just playing along with him?"

"He thinks I'm teasing." Tammy impatiently pushed her hat off her head and it settled on her back, held in place with a string around her neck. "I want to tell him that I'm very serious, but I'm so afraid that he'll totally reject me." She looked at Elizabeth with tears in her eyes. "Oh, Libby! I love him so much! I want him to be my husband. I want to stay here with him forever!"

"Oh, Tammy, Tammy." Sweet Water tossed her head up and down and Elizabeth gripped the reins tighter. "Tammy, I don't want you to be hurt. You'll be going home in two weeks, and then what?"

"No. No, Elizabeth. I'm staying here. I'm going to give Nolen a chance to love me. You said that we have equal right to Sandhill Ranch. I can stay here."

"But what will you do for money? How will you live?"

"Mark works in town and drives back and forth except in the worst part of winter. I can do the same." Tammy's eyes narrowed. "I think Mark likes you a lot, Libby. Why don't you stay and see if it'll develop into love?"

Her eyes flew open wide and she gasped. "You've got to be kidding! What about my career? I'd never give it up. And can you see the young rancher Mark McCall giving up all of this to travel around with me?"

Tammy laughed and shook her head. "No. I guess you're right. He likes working on the ranch as well as working in town selling machinery."

"I think Mark likes a girl at church. Did you notice that girl with the long black hair when we were there on Sunday? She was dressed in a white dress with tiny yellow roses."

"I saw her talking with Vickie, but I didn't notice

Mark with her." Tammy suddenly pointed down the hill. "Here comes Nolen! Oh, my heart!"

Elizabeth sighed and shook her head. "You didn't hear a word I said, did you?"

"Be happy for me, Libby! I'm in love for the first time in my life! All those years when I chased boys and they chased me, I never really fell in love. Just being with Nolen makes me happy. I feel alive!" She nudged Peaches forward and soon joined Nolen.

Elizabeth waved to them, then shouted, "I'll meet you back at the ranch." They lifted their hands to her in a wave, then rode off slowly side by side, finally disappearing behind a grassy knoll. "Oh, Tammy, Tammy. I don't want you to be hurt."

After several minutes she rode toward the ranch, Sweet Water picking his own trail. Suddenly the big bay lifted his head and nickered as if he'd seen another horse. Elizabeth looked around thoughtfully, but saw nothing except a cottontail hopping out of sight.

Sweet Water nickered again, bobbing his head, and Elizabeth knew another horse was near.

"Let's check it out, Sweet Water." Elizabeth nudged the horse forward around a clump of cottonwood trees, then stopped. A saddled horse stood grazing beside the trees and a girl lay face down on the grass under the tree, and her body shook with sobs.

"It's Vickie," whispered Elizabeth as she quickly dismounted and dropped the reins to the ground. Why was Vickie crying? She had looked very pale and unhappy lately, but her mother had said nothing was wrong.

Elizabeth remembered how Vickie had chased Kevin and Toby until she caught them and then she'd hug and

47

kiss them. Now she was twenty years old, no longer a little girl.

"Vickie." Elizabeth spoke softly and Vickie jerked up, dabbing at her tears.

"I . . . I didn't hear you." Vickie sniffed hard. "I must look a mess. I don't usually fling myself on the grass and cry." She picked a leaf from her long dark hair and let it drop to the ground.

"I'll help if I can, Vickie. Will you talk to me? You can trust me."

Fresh tears filled Vickie's dark eyes and she turned away, her head down. "I can't talk right now."

"Then let's just sit down for a while. I want to be with you and let you know I care. We don't have to talk." Elizabeth touched Vickie's arm and finally Vickie sat down and Elizabeth sat beside her. "You look as if you've been crying a long time."

"It feels as if it's been all my life."

"I can remember you as a little girl of eight. You were bubbly and full of life and loved everyone, especially my two brothers. You are still a tiny girl, but I know you're grown up. I think you're shorter than my sister Susan. You do know Susan has a baby girl, don't you? She's a year old and has red hair. And she can walk already. Mom and Dad love her to pieces."

"Your family is special, Libby." She sighed and shook her head. "I don't know if I can remember to call you Elizabeth."

"That's all right." Elizabeth picked a piece of grass and stripped it with her fingernail. "Ben and Jill are going to have a baby soon, at least by the end of July. They're really excited and anxious."

"Are you going to marry and have babies?"

"Someday. Are you?"

Vickie burst into tears again and her shoulders shook with sobs.

Elizabeth gathered her close and sat with her until finally she pulled away and wiped her tears. Her nose and eyes were red and she sniffed hard. Elizabeth blinked away tears of her own. Vickie looked very, very unhappy.

"Libby, Jock Anders and I were going to be married this summer. He said he'd set the date for sure this month." Vickie's voice quivered and she locked her fingers together. "But now he says he's not ready to settle down. He says he found another girl. He called several days ago and said he was leaving and that it was good-bye forever! And he took that girl with him!"

"Oh, Vickie, I am so sorry! I'm glad you didn't marry him. He doesn't sound like the forever type. And you shouldn't settle for anything less. God has the perfect man for you, Vickie. You'll see."

"It's so hard to face everyone here. All my friends knew that we were planning to get married. And now they feel sorry for me. I can't stand it! I wish I could run away, but I'm too old to run away. I'm not a child. I'm twenty years old. Some of my friends are married with kids already." She covered her face. "I can't go on this way!"

Elizabeth gently tugged Vickie's hands down. "Come home with me. You can stay as long as you want, and then when you come home your friends will have other things to think about. And you'll have other things to think about, too." Elizabeth laughed.

"Kevin and Toby would love to have you chase them around again."

She laughed between sniffs. "Wasn't I terrible?"

"You were adorable and you still are." Elizabeth smiled. "What do you say? Will you come home with me?"

"What will your parents say?"

"I'll call them and ask them, but I know they'll love to have you."

"But you already have a houseful."

Elizabeth sighed. "I'm afraid to say this, but Tammy is going to stay here. She doesn't want to leave Nebraska."

Vickie pushed her long hair back. "Nolen will be glad of that. He loves her."

"He does? Are you sure?"

"I know Nolen Brown. I know when he's teasing and when he's serious, and he is serious about Tammy. But he thinks she's teasing him. He doesn't think she cares about him."

"She does," said Elizabeth softly. "She loves him." She jumped up and held her hand out to pull up Vickie. "I think it's time to give those two a helping hand."

Vickie laughed and color returned to her face. "I think you're right. And I know just the thing."

"What? What?" Elizabeth reached for the dangling reins and held them as she waited excitedly for Vickie's answer.

"We'll invite the minister over for supper and we'll tell him that Nolen and Tammy are getting married and they want him to perform the ceremony."

Elizabeth shook her head. "No! We couldn't do that!"

"Watch and see, my girl. Watch and see." Vickie

swung into the saddle and bumped her horse with her knees.

Elizabeth followed Vickie, trying to decide if Vickie was joking or serious. At the corral she jumped off Sweet Water and caught Vickie's arm. "You aren't serious, are you?"

Vickie laughed and her dark eyes sparkled with mischief. "I sure am! And why not? Aren't they asking for it? Hasn't Nolen needed a joke played on him? He's worse than the rest of us with the practical jokes. He doesn't know when to quit. Now, he'll know." Vickie shook her finger at Elizabeth. "And don't you dare tell either one of them! Do you hear?"

Elizabeth rolled her eyes and shook her head. "All right. I won't tell, but please put a stop to it if it's going to hurt someone."

"It won't hurt a single person because *I* know Nolen loves Tammy and *you* know that Tammy loves Nolen." She pulled the saddle off her horse, then the bridle and turned him into the corral. Finally Elizabeth did the same with Sweet Water.

"When are you going to call your folks about me going home with you?" Vickie walked toward the small house with Elizabeth. Elizabeth felt like a giant next to the short girl.

"I'll call right away."

"I'll run in and grab a shower, then come to your place and hear what they said."

"Don't be nervous about it, Vickie. I know they'll agree."

"I won't feel badly if they don't."

The corners of her mouth drooped and Elizabeth knew she'd feel worse than before. Elizabeth squeezed Vickie's arm. "You'll see. Come back later."

Vickie looped her thumbs in her belt and stood with her small booted feet apart. "I can handle whatever way it goes."

"It'll go our way."

Vickie stood very still, then finally turned and ran to the larger house several yards away.

Elizabeth walked into Nolen's house and tossed her hat onto the hook at the back door. She tugged off her boots and set them neatly on the floor under the hook. With a sigh she sat on the chair next to the phone and dialed the home number. Her heart raced as she realized that Badden could be sitting beside one of the phones.

When he answered, her mouth dried and her heart almost leaped out of her rib cage. "Hello, Badden."

"Elizabeth! How's your vacation? Are you coming home?"

He missed her! He was glad to hear from her! She clung to the receiver. "Tammy and I are enjoying ourselves and I'll be home when I said I would." Why couldn't she hop a plane and go now? Had Badden changed? He sounded different—younger and happier. "Is Toby helping you with riding and swimming?"

"Yes. We get along very well. I have some wonderful news for you."

"What?" She held her breath.

"Your dad has been showing me Scriptures on being born again and two days ago I accepted Jesus as my personal Savior."

"Oh, Badden," she whispered as tears rushed down her cheeks. "I am so glad! Thank God!"

"Are you crying?"

"Yes. Because I'm so happy for you."

"I'm happy for me, too. I have a purpose in life now. I

feel complete. I thought often about what you said about the empty God-shaped space inside me, and finally I understood."

"Oh, Badden!" She wanted to see his face while he was telling her. She wanted to touch him to know that she wasn't dreaming.

"Come home, Elizabeth. I miss you."

Her pulse leaped. "You do?"

"Of course. You're the first friend I've ever had."

Friend? But of course. What else could he mean? And she wanted only friendship from him. She didn't have time for a deeper relationship and neither did he. "I'll be back by the tenth."

"I'll meet you at the airport."

She slumped in her chair and closed her eyes. "It's not necessary. Dad's going to. It's all arranged." She knew she sounded very brisk and businesslike, but she couldn't help it. "Is Mom there? Could I speak to her?"

He was quiet awhile. "I'll get Vera."

She heard him lay the phone down and then in a few minutes Vera spoke. After they talked several minutes Elizabeth said, "Mom, Vickie needs to get away awhile. Is it all right if she comes home with me to spend time with us?"

"Certainly, honey. We'll be glad to have her. Kevin is gone on a case and he said he might not be back for several weeks. She can have his room."

"Tammy is staying here, so Vickie could always share my room."

"Tammy's staying?"

Elizabeth quickly explained, then added, "Don't say anything to the others in case she changes her mind. She wouldn't want to explain what was happening."

Just as they were ready to say good-bye Vera asked, "Did you say something to hurt Badden? He looks as if he's lost his best friend."

"He'll be all right, Mom. Tell him 'bye for me and I'll see you the week after next."

Elizabeth sat very still after she hung up, and tears slowly slipped down her cheeks and splashed onto her folded hands.

SIX
Nebraska wedding

The following Saturday Elizabeth walked into the
kitchen where Lou McCall was cooking supper for the
minister and his wife. "May I help, Lou?"

Lou turned with a smile, a large fork in her hand. She
looked like an older version of Vickie. "I'm finishing the
chicken and the potatoes will be done soon. You can
mash them if you want."

Elizabeth leaned against the counter near the sink
and watched Lou turn the pieces of chicken in the cast
iron skillet. "I'm glad you and Brad agreed to Vickie's
going back with me."

"She needs a little freedom right now, and we want
her to have it. She needs to know that there is more to
life than what's here. And that there are more men
around. I never did like Jock Anders. He wasn't her
type. I'm glad he's gone. But I hate to see Vickie's heart
broken over him."

Lou drained the potatoes and the steam rose around
her, then she set the pot of potatoes on a hotpad on the

counter and handed Elizabeth a round potato-masher. "I'll get the butter and milk for you."

Elizabeth mashed the potatoes, glancing at the clock every few minutes. Pastor Clark and his wife would be here soon and then Vickie would tell them that Nolen and Tammy were planning to marry.

Lou set the bowl of salad on the counter, then reached for the dressing. "I'm glad Vickie thought to have a special time with Pastor before she leaves."

Elizabeth mashed harder, willing her face to stay normal and not turn bright red.

By the time supper was over and everyone had visited for quite a while, Elizabeth began to breathe easier. Vickie had been teasing. She hadn't intended to say anything to Pastor Clark about Nolen and Tammy. Elizabeth looked at the white-haired man and his plump wife and hid a smile behind her hand.

Just then Pastor Clark looked over at Nolen and Tammy sitting hand in hand on the couch and said, "So, you two are planning a wedding."

Elizabeth forced back a gasp and Nolen and Tammy stared at the pastor then at each other in surprise.

"I know you're both fine Christians, so there isn't any reason why we can't set a date as soon as you want it. Even next week is all right if you want it and Vickie seemed to think you might."

Nolen shot a look at Vickie, then smiled. "Next week will be fine."

Elizabeth choked and Vickie almost toppled off her chair.

"How about it, Tammy?" asked Nolen, holding her hand to his heart. "Is that too soon for you?"

Her face paled and she tried to smile. She looked hopelessly at Elizabeth.

"If you agree to next week, then I can be at the wedding," Elizabeth said, hoping that those words would make Tammy realize that Nolen wasn't just joking.

Tammy looked into Nolen's face and whispered huskily, "I'll marry you whenever you say. I mean it!"

He looked at her and his eyes widened, then he jumped up, pulling her to her feet. "I have a few private words I want to say to you." He rushed her to the door, then looked back at Vickie questioningly.

"Just so they're love words, Nolen," Vickie said with a grin.

Nolen winked and whisked Tammy away and Elizabeth sank back in her chair, suddenly feeling too weak to move.

Lou shook her head and Brad said, "Well, I'll be. I didn't know those two were that serious."

Elizabeth couldn't say anything. She listened to the others talk while she waited nervously for Tammy and Nolen to walk back in.

When they did, Tammy looked as if she'd been thoroughly kissed and Nolen kept his arm possessively around her. They stopped in front of Pastor Clark. "Friday morning at nine o'clock we'll all be at the church for you to marry us. Elizabeth and Mark will be our witnesses, and only the family will attend."

"That sounds very organized," the pastor said as he stood up and shook hands with Nolen. "My wife will play the organ."

Much later Elizabeth sat on the couch in Nolen's house and shivered as she thought about how Vickie's plan could have backfired. When the door opened and

Tammy walked in, her face beaming and her hair mussed, Elizabeth relaxed. Everything was all right.

"I am so happy!" Tammy twirled around the small room, almost bumping into the table. "Elizabeth, my dream has come true! I am going to marry the most wonderful man in the entire world!" Suddenly she stopped right in front of Elizabeth. "Were you in on the joke with the pastor?"

"Well . . . I . . . ." Her voice faded away and she spread out her hands and hunched her shoulders.

"You knew! I thought so! Thank you! I wouldn't have been able to tell Nolen that I really loved him if you hadn't said what you did. I took from it that you'd learned that he really did love me."

"Vickie told me."

Tammy dropped to the couch and caught Elizabeth's hands. "He said he honestly did fall for me when he saw me at the airport. He wasn't joking. But he said he had to treat it as a joke so that I wouldn't hurt him if I didn't care for him. Oh, but I love him! I told him that and he said that there was no reason why we shouldn't get married. He said he'd marry me tonight if he could, and I told him I felt the same. I just wish your family could be here."

"What will your mother say if you don't invite her?"

Tammy jumped up, her hands clenched at her sides, her eyes wide. "I don't want her here! What would Nolen say if he knew I had a mother like Phyllis LaDere?"

"He loves you. He wouldn't judge you by your mother. But you do what you want. I know God will help you act in love."

Tammy nodded slowly, then walked to the phone and dialed her mother's number. Elizabeth started toward her room, but Tammy asked her to please stay. She sank back down on the couch and locked her suddenly icy fingers together. When Tammy finally spoke to her mother, Elizabeth's stomach cramped painfully. Phyllis must not do or say anything to dim Tammy's happiness!

Silently Elizabeth prayed for Tammy and for Phyllis. Finally Tammy hung up and walked to the couch, a surprised look on her face.

"She's happy for me. She said she's glad that I love him. She's going to come to the wedding if she can. And she said she'd send me money to buy a wedding gown. She said since she never wore one, she wanted me to have one."

"Do you think your mother really did love our father?" asked Elizabeth in a hushed voice.

"I know that she never married. She lived with a lot of men, but she never married any of them. I don't understand my mother, and maybe I never will."

They talked for several minutes then Tammy said, "It's too late tonight to call your family, but will you call them in the morning before church? I want them to know about my marriage."

Elizabeth thought about Badden answering the phone and she said, "You call them, Tammy. I know they'd want to congratulate you themselves."

The next day when Tammy called, Chuck and Vera said they'd hop a plane and be there for the wedding. "Chuck, will you give me away then?" Tears sparkled in Tammy's blue eyes.

"It will be my privilege, Tammy. We'll see you Thursday sometime, and we'll fly back Saturday with Elizabeth and Vickie."

"We're happy for you, Tammy," said Vera softly. "Nolen is a fine young man."

Thursday afternoon Elizabeth parked at the airport and slid out of the McCalls' station wagon. She slipped her sunglasses up to the top of her head as she walked into the shade of the small building. Her white and pink sundress swished around her legs. Today was not as hot and windy as usual.

She wanted to run instead of walk to the back where she knew she was to wait for the small plane to land. Soon she'd see her parents. Dare she ask about Badden? Would they think she had fallen in love with him?

A man and woman stood at the window and she called to them and flung her arms around Chuck, and then Vera. "You're early!" she cried as she looked at them, then hugged them again.

"We've been waiting just a few minutes," said Vera. She was dressed in pale yellow slacks and matching knit top. "It's good to be in Nebraska again."

"Especially for a wedding," said Chuck as he nodded his red head. The laugh lines deepened around his eyes as he chuckled. "Just so it's not your wedding."

Elizabeth clapped her hand to her heart, her hazel eyes wide. "Mine! I won't marry until I'm at least thirty-five!"

"Hello, Elizabeth."

She spun around at the quiet voice behind her, then just stared up at Badden, her mouth gaping.

"I am not a ghost," he said with a dry laugh. "I can't tell by your face if you're glad to see me or absolutely terrified."

She closed her mouth and swallowed hard, then

looked at her parents, then back at Badden. "I didn't know you were coming."

"I decided at the last minute that I'd like to. I wanted to see what fascination Nebraska held for you."

Her legs felt like rubber and she was sure he could hear her heart hammering wildly. "Tammy will be pleased that you're here for the wedding. Will you play the wedding march for her?"

"If she wants."

Why was he looking at her so intently? What did he want of her? Was he still fearful that she'd fall in love with him? Abruptly she turned to Chuck and gripped his arm. "Let's hurry to the car and get to the church. They are going to have a brief practice so that we'll all know what to do in the morning."

"Just think, a few hours ago we were home," said Vera. "I think I like flying. But I didn't like the small plane very well."

Chuck stopped at the back of the wagon and Elizabeth unlocked it. "Vera gripped the arms of the seat so tightly that she left her finger marks behind," he said as he set their luggage in.

"I saw you flinch a couple of times, Chuck," said Vera, nudging him.

"But our friend Badden here took it all in stride," said Chuck, patting Badden's back. "Not a single air pocket bothered him."

Badden smiled. "I had my mind on other things." He held the door open for Elizabeth and she slid under the steering wheel. He walked around and slid in beside her while Chuck and Vera sat in the back.

Elizabeth drove toward the church in a daze. Badden's presence in the seat beside her almost overwhelmed her and she refused to think why. He was here and she had to live with it.

Inside the small church she hurried to Tammy's side and left her parents to introduce Badden to the others. "Tammy, Badden came," she whispered.

Tammy smiled and waved to him, then hurried to him. "Will you please play the wedding march and another song for us, Badden? Is that imposing too much?"

He took her hands, then kissed her cheek. "Not at all, Tammy. I'll be glad to do it for you."

"Thank you." Tammy excused herself and rushed to find Nolen, saying she wanted to tell him.

Elizabeth saw Mark near a door just off the platform and she hurried to him away from Badden. "Hi. Are you all set for tomorrow?"

He took a deep breath. "I'd feel more at home outdoors on the ranch, but I reckon I can walk down the aisle with you without falling flat on my face."

"If I hang on too tightly, don't mind me." She smiled at him and he smiled back, looking very handsome in his Western plaid shirt and jeans.

"Nolen's parents won't come to the wedding," said Mark in a low voice close to Elizabeth's ear. "He felt pretty down about it, but he soon got over it. They said they gave him up years ago, and he has a life of his own and so do they. But the Davises are coming. Holly and her husband said they wouldn't miss it. Remember how Holly and Nolen used to fight? Not only are they cousins, but they're best friends now."

"I'm glad." She peeked at Badden and he was frowning at her. She asked Mark about Holly's brother, Aaron, and Mark told her, but his words pounded against her and didn't sink in. Why didn't Badden stop looking at her? If she were beautiful like Vickie then he'd have something to look at, but she was tall and thin and not at all beautiful.

After practice Badden insisted on staying in town at a motel and she drove listlessly to the ranch with her parents. She managed to carry on a conversation until they reached Nolen's small house. "Mom and Dad, you sleep here where I've been sleeping. I'm going to double up with Tammy tonight."

"This is a pretty little house," said Vera as she looked around. "Nolen and Tammy should be very happy here."

"Did you see a lawyer about this property?" asked Chuck.

Elizabeth nodded. "Tammy and I went to one in town, so now we both own the portion of Sandhill Ranch that Frank Dobbs left to me. And Nolen owns what Old Zeb had. That really puts it in the family, doesn't it?" She managed to laugh, wondering how she could talk when her thoughts were trying to stray to Badden. Why had he come?

"The others said to say hello," said Vera to Elizabeth. "Jill said to tell you that she'd wait until you got home before she has the baby. The doctor says any day, though, so I told them to call us if she goes into the hospital."

"I want to be with her," said Elizabeth as she sat on the edge of the couch. "I wouldn't want to miss it."

The next morning, she thought about Jill off and on, but the wedding pushed Jill to the back of her mind. She looked at the pale orange dress that floated down around her feet, then clung tightly to Mark's arm as they walked down the aisle. She peeked at Badden at the piano but he was totally involved in the music. She missed her step and Mark pressed her hand. She wanted to stand beside Badden and listen to the music without thinking of anything else. Her heart almost burst to see him at the piano again. Oh, he dare not give up piano!

She stood in place and watched Tammy walk down the aisle with Chuck. Phyllis LaDere had not come after all, and she hadn't sent money, but Tammy had said it didn't matter. She'd found a simple satin gown in white when she'd shopped in the closest city a few days ago. Her hair was caught up and baby's breath was entwined in it. Tammy looked beautiful and Elizabeth saw the look on Nolen's face and knew he agreed. Chuck handed Tammy to Nolen and Badden played "Our Love Is Forever."

Tears stung her eyes as she looked at him. The music wrapped around her and her heart swelled with love. With his music he could make her feel whatever he wanted her to and she wondered if he knew it.

She watched as Tammy and Nolen exchanged vows, then rings. She caught Mark's eyes and smiled. Would Mark be the next to marry?

Much later Elizabeth stood outside the church beside Mark and waved to Tammy and Nolen as they drove away. Elizabeth dabbed away a few tears, then looked up at Mark. "That was a beautiful wedding. Thank you for being in it. It meant a lot to Tammy. She is happy that she's going to be a part of this community and this church and your family."

"We welcome any sister of yours, Libby," said Mark softly. "You have a special place in our hearts, and you always will have." He pulled her close and kissed her gently.

She touched his face. "You're a good friend, Mark.

And I love you." She turned her head as someone brushed past her. Badden's face was as white as the clouds in the sky. He glared at her, then walked briskly to join Chuck and Vera with the McCalls.

"Your friend can really play the piano well," said Mark as he followed her look.

"He plays concert piano," she said in a low, tight voice. "He is brilliant."

Mark slipped his arm around her shoulder. "And so are you, Elizabeth Gail Johnson. You know the eight-track tape you sent me? I play it all the time. Someday I'm going to attend one of your concerts and see you live. And I'll tell everyone around that I knew you when."

She leaned her head into his shoulder, cheered by his words. If she could get on an easy footing with Badden again, she'd be happy.

SEVEN
Family crisis

Elizabeth paced Chuck's study from the window to the large oak desk to the leather couch, then back again. Why was Badden avoiding her? They'd been home from Nebraska almost two weeks already and he'd made sure that he was never alone with her. He preferred being with Toby and Vickie or even Peggy and Alan.

Abruptly Elizabeth stopped near the bookcase, her fists clenched tightly, her head down. Her long, brown hair cascaded down to hide her face. What had she done to offend Badden? She lifted her head and her eyes widened.

Did he think she'd fallen in love with him? Was he protecting himself from her?

She nervously fingered the butterfly necklace at her throat, then rubbed her hands down her jeans. He couldn't think that. She'd kept her actions friendly, and just a little cool.

She heard a step at the door and she knew it was Badden before she looked by the strange little leaps of her heart. Finally she turned to face him, and she even managed a smile.

His dark eyes were almost black as he stepped closer to her. His presence filled the room and he seemed to tower over her. He was dressed in a tan tee shirt and this was the first time she'd ever seen him in jeans. He stopped and he was close enough that his breath touched her face and she shivered.

"I've been watching you for days," he said in a low tense voice. "And each day the sadness grows in you and I can no longer tolerate it."

She faced him squarely, quivering inside. "*You* can't? What have I to do with you?"

"You are part of my life and you know it."

She could see the flecks of light brown in his dark brown eyes. "I don't know any such thing!"

He gripped her arms and his touch burned her skin and she tried to pull free, but he was stronger. "You forced yourself on me by siding with Marv Secord, so now you must pay for it. You brought me here and you showed me a life I never knew existed outside of books or TV. And now that I'm here, I have the right to know why you're walking around like a lonely shadow. Why haven't you been practicing? And why haven't you laughed in four days?"

She swallowed and bit the inside of her bottom lip, her eyes down.

He slipped his hand under her hair and around her slender neck and rubbed the butterfly necklace with his thumb. His other hand circled her waist and her heart thudded painfully. She wanted to look up at him to read his expression, but she couldn't move.

He lifted her chin with his thumb as his sensitive

fingers curled into her hair. She raised her eyes only to the level of his wide mouth and she knew he was going to kiss her.

His lips were soft, and then demanding and she clung to him.

Finally he held her from him and she lifted her heavy lids to look at him. There was a strange expression on his face—a mixture of anger and pain.

"That should hold you until your cowboy can come see you." He dropped his hands and strode out the door, closing it with a sharp click.

Her legs gave way and she sank down on the couch, trembling hands at her mouth, hazel eyes staring blankly at the closed door. What did he mean? Why had he kissed her?

She covered her pale face. Never in her life had a kiss affected her that way. Was her body trying to tell her that it was time for love for her?

How could she face Badden again? She groaned. Tonight they were having a party and all her friends were coming and they'd expect to see her smiling and happy with Badden nearby. How could she have a party to introduce all her friends to Badden? Just seeing him would remind her of what had happened between them. And it would remind him of her passionate surrender. What must he think of her?

Just then the door burst open and Peggy dashed in, then stopped dead. "Oh, I'm sorry, Elizabeth. I thought the study was empty. I wanted to use the phone."

Elizabeth looked up at the girl dressed in shorts and suntop and forced a smile. "I'll give you some privacy, then."

"Are you all set for the party tonight?" Peggy lifted

herself to the large oak desk and sat on it with her ankles crossed and her hands pressed on the desk on either side of her.

"I have a few things to do. Are you ready for your guitar solo?"

Peggy's dark eyes twinkled. "I am going to surprise a few people. I hope Toby will notice that I'm not a little girl like he thinks." Her face clouded over. "Why did you have to bring Vickie McCall here? She takes all of Toby's attention. And I don't like that at all!"

Elizabeth laughed gently. "Peggy, Toby is much too old for you." Elizabeth could hear those same words as an echo in her memory when she'd thought she loved Scott Norris. "Don't be jealous of Vickie, honey, because it's a waste of your energy. Toby is good for Vickie. She needs a friend now, and he needs some play time after working so hard in college the past four years."

Peggy wrinkled her small nose. "I know you're right. I just wish she wasn't quite so pretty."

Elizabeth knew just how Peggy felt. "But, Peggy, you're pretty, too. You have beautiful brown hair and big brown eyes and a figure that would put Miss Universe to shame."

"Oh, sure." She hopped off the desk and grinned at Elizabeth. "I wish you'd make a recording of that so I could play it to my mirror."

Elizabeth hugged her, then walked out of the study feeling much better. She sat at her baby grand and played with passion and fire. The piano was an old friend and always seemed to understand her feelings.

Later she walked outdoors and let the gentle wind blow against her. She stopped at the pen beside the horse barn and Snowball nickered and came to nuzzle her shoulder. The white foal at Snowball's side neighed in her shrill way, then ran across the pen, then back to Snowball's side. Elizabeth laughed and reached out to touch the little white ball of fluff. She looked just as Snowball had at that age. And the Johnsons had known Elizabeth loved Snowball, so they'd given her to her for her twelfth birthday.

Snowball had grown up and had had seven foals, all of them white, except one. He'd been dark red.

Elizabeth pressed her face against Snowball's neck. It smelled dusty. "We've seen a lot of life together, you and I. I miss you when I'm gone."

Slowly Elizabeth walked into the barn. She'd spent many hours cleaning it, along with her other chores. She sat on a bale of hay and remembered the time April and May Brakie had run away from their foster home and hid in the barn until she'd agreed to help them. Tonight they were coming to the party—Adam and April Feuder, Joe and May Wilkens. Both girls had small babies.

She heard voices outside the barn and she walked to the door to see Toby and Badden and Vickie dismounting near the fence.

"That was fun," said Vickie in her slow drawl. "You have a lovely farm, Toby."

His face turned red and almost blotted out the freckles that merged into his red hair. "Thanks, Vickie."

"I think the Christmas tree business is a great idea," said Badden as he leaned against the fence, the reins loosely in his hands. "Alan must really enjoy it."

Toby nodded, then explained how Ben had started the business years ago, then Kevin had taken it over and finally he himself, and now Alan.

Badden listened attentively, nodding occasionally. His blond hair had been cut neatly and his skin had darkened from the sun.

Elizabeth stood hidden inside the barn and watched Badden's every movement, every expression. A flame of love leaped inside her. She stood very still, her eyes wide, her hands at her sides. She loved him!

She loved him!

She swallowed hard and shook her head. No. It wasn't possible. But the love burned inside her and wouldn't die down and couldn't be extinguished and she finally had to admit that it was true.

She was in love with Badden Lindsay.

How insipid that sounded. And her feelings were far from insipid. She could understand how Tammy felt about Nolen. Elizabeth shook her head helplessly. It couldn't happen to her. She had a successful career. She had everything.

But what would it all mean without Badden?

She peeked out at him and she wondered how he could stand there as if nothing had happened. Why didn't he feel that she was nearby, that love was streaming out from her to him? Why didn't he look at her and realize that he loved her?

Her shoulders drooped. He had said that he didn't want love, that he had nothing to give. He had forbidden her to fall in love with him. If he learned that she had, he would leave and she'd never see him again. And if the others knew that she loved Badden and wasn't loved in return, they would feel sorry for her and she couldn't bear that.

She had to hide her feelings from him. If she walked out and faced him now he'd be able to read her love. She needed time to build a wall, a wall like the one Badden had around him.

Quietly she walked to the back door of the barn and slipped out. She stopped near a large oak and leaned against it out of sight.

She loved Badden Lindsay!

She closed her eyes and gently touched her lips as she remembered his kisses. If only he'd meant them! But she couldn't think of that. She had to build a wall around herself brick by brick and she would do it. She'd learned how as an unloved child and she would do it again.

That evening she walked outdoors in her dark red swimsuit with the lighter red coverup and she felt protected behind the invisible coverup she'd placed over her feelings. Peggy had said that several people were already there at the pool and she'd hurried out, ready to face even Badden.

Susan waved to her and she waved back.

Badden stood beside the pool dressed only in swim trunks and he was talking to a blonde girl with a gorgeous figure. Elizabeth frowned and when the girl turned, Elizabeth froze. The girl was Joanne Tripper, her enemy from high school who was also a concert pianist now.

She laughed up at Badden and he laughed also. Jealousy ripped through Elizabeth and she wanted to push Joanne and her fantastic body into the pool.

Badden stepped toward Elizabeth. "I met a friend in town this afternoon and I invited her to the party. I knew you wouldn't mind."

"Hello, Libby," said Joanne coldly.

"Joanne." Elizabeth unclenched her fists and tried to smile. "I hope you'll make yourself right at home."

Joanne looked up at Badden and batted her inch-long lashes. "Oh, I will."

Elizabeth turned away and rushed to meet Jill and Ben as they walked toward the pool from around the garage.

"I don't think I'll get much swimming done," said Jill as she laughingly touched her stomach. "I feel out of place with all the slim people around."

"You look prettier than any of them," said Ben, kissing her cheek. "You be sure to tell me if your contractions start."

"I will, Ben. But I know I'll be all right. I think Toby's trying to get your attention. I'll find a chair and sit down with Elizabeth awhile."

"You take care of her, Elizabeth," said Ben, looking worried as he rubbed his hand across his red hair. "The doctor said she should've had the baby last week."

"I'll take care of her, Ben. Don't worry." Elizabeth squeezed his hand and he smiled, then hurried to talk to Toby. They looked like real brothers with the same red hair, but Toby had been adopted when he was nine years old.

"I see Joanne managed to crash another party," said Jill in a low voice as they walked slowly toward the chairs around the deck.

"Badden brought her. He has no idea that she gave us such fits in school."

"He's really enjoying her, isn't he?" Jill frowned and Elizabeth couldn't bring herself to look at the two.

Jill turned to sit and her ankle twisted and she fell heavily to the concrete deck, crying out with pain. Elizabeth shouted for Ben, then dropped beside Jill.

"Don't move! Just let us see if you hurt yourself or the baby." She looked up frantically for Ben but Badden was there instead. He knelt beside her and caught her hand, then asked Jill if she thought anything was broken or harmed.

"I don't know," said Jill with a sob. "Where's Ben?"

"Jill!" Ben dropped at her side and touched her face and touched her stomach. "Oh, Jill! I'm going to carefully help you up."

She moaned and Elizabeth gripped Badden's hand tightly.

"I'm going to take her to the hospital," said Ben. "Elizabeth, you get her suitcase and follow us in, please. She might not have to stay, but I want to be prepared."

"I'll get it." Elizabeth stood up and Badden's arm wrapped firmly around her, holding her against him as Ben carefully helped Jill to stand.

"I do think I'm all right," Jill said in an unsteady voice.

"We'll meet you at the hospital, Elizabeth," Ben said as he helped Jill to walk.

Elizabeth asked Susan to take care of the party. "I don't know when I'll be back. I'm sorry for leaving everyone this way." She tried to pull away from Badden, but his hand tightened.

"I'm driving you," he said. "We are both going to get dressed, and then I'm taking you in."

She shook her head. "It's not necessary. I can manage. Oh, I wish Mom and Dad were home!"

"Don't argue, Elizabeth!" Badden firmly guided her into the house and up the stairs. He gently pushed her into her room. "Just pull on jeans and a shirt. I'll be right back."

Helplessly she looked around, then jerked open her drawer and pulled out jeans. She grabbed a blouse out of the closet and slipped it on, buttoning it as Badden joined her, his shirttail out. She pushed her feet into her sandals and Badden knelt and buckled them. She touched his soft hair and said, "You don't have to take me in. Really. I'll be all right."

He caught her hand and rushed downstairs to his silver Mercedes and she sat beside him, fear squeezing her heart.

"Jill will be all right and so will the baby," said Badden as he pulled onto the road. "We have a good God who loves them and will take care of them."

Elizabeth sniffed loudly and nodded.

Badden stopped at Ben's small house. "Where's Jill's suitcase. Tell me and I'll get it."

She slipped from the car and ran with him to the door. She pulled the extra key from under the cactus plant and opened the door and they rushed in.

Badden grabbed the case, then pulled Elizabeth close. "Your friend will be all right. You must believe that."

She clung to him thankfully, then hurried to the car.

EIGHT
A new Johnson

Elizabeth huddled against Badden, her eyes glued on the closed door leading to the delivery room of the maternity ward.

"Please relax, Elizabeth. You don't want to be sick and miss out on the news of a new niece or nephew."

"They've been in there so long!"

"But the nurse said that the labor was going along normally, that the fall didn't harm Jill or the baby. She said Jill's contractions would have started anyway." Badden gently lifted her head, his long sensitive fingers on her pale cheek, his thumb under her chin. She looked at him, her hazel eyes moist with unshed tears. "Elizabeth, babies are born every day. You were born. I was born. Jill will be all right."

She trembled and forced herself to pull away from him. "I don't mean to be such a child."

"Come back here." He pulled her close again and she could feel his heart beating against her.

"Oh, I wonder what is going on in there! I'm glad Ben is in the delivery room with Jill." Elizabeth's sigh

came out in a shiver and she looked up into Badden's face. "Did Dad say they'd be here?"

Badden shook his head. "He said that they're needed at home to give comfort there. But they'll come if we need them." He tapped the tip of her nose with a long, thin finger. "Now stop worrying."

A smile trembled on her lips and she closed her eyes. His right arm tightened around her and with his left hand he smoothed back her hair.

"Would you like to hear about my childhood, Elizabeth?"

She nodded against him as she spread her fingers over his heart. She felt it leap, then settle into a steady rhythm.

"I was an only child, shy and backward except when it came to music. Mother played the piano and she taught me the notes before I started school. My dad left us when I was about seven and Mother poured her life into me."

Elizabeth looked at him in sympathy, but he was staring off into space.

"She said that I was going to become *someone*—not like Dad. She chose piano for me since I had a natural talent for it. And she worked with me constantly. I wanted to play with the boys in the neighborhood but she wouldn't allow it. She said I was *special* and I couldn't waste my years as the others were doing. Year after year I studied piano with different teachers. She thought of sending me to Julliard, but she found another school that had a teacher whom she knew was someone."

Elizabeth moved her hand up until her fingers touched the bare column of his neck. He smiled and leaned his head slightly toward her.

"As soon as I performed in front of a group of music lovers I was hooked. Then I wanted piano for myself, for the applause and the acceptance. I made piano my entire life, and when Mother died it was barely a loss for me."

His voice rose and fell and she listened with her heart open, loving him as a boy, then a teen, and as an adult.

For a long while he was quiet and then he lifted her face and looked into her eyes. "Tell me about you."

She shrank from him, her eyes round. "No, No, Badden," she whispered.

"Please." He rubbed his fingertip over her lips and it was as if he'd touched his mouth to hers. "Please."

She pulled away from him but he kept her hand imprisoned in his. She tugged, but he wouldn't release her so she gave up and left it there. She looked down at the well-polished floor, then at him, lifting her chin defensively. "My mother was Marie Dobbs. My father, Frank Dobbs, left us when I was three. He's Tammy's father, too. Our mothers are sisters." She bit her bottom lip and looked away. "I won't go into detail but I ended up in one foster home after another until the Johnsons prayed me into their family. I was adopted and I found a family's love as well as God's love and I learned piano. But I didn't start until I was eleven. After high school I attended Maddox School of Music." She smiled briefly at him. "And I first met you three years ago. I heard you play at Grace Hall and I couldn't wait to meet you in person. You had been my hero for years."

"Hero!" He laughed and shook his head.

"Yes, hero. And I walked backstage to tell you how much I enjoyed your music, and that someday I wanted to play as well as you. But . . ." She wrinkled her nose and looked away, but he caught her chin and pulled her to face him again. "But when you shook my hand everything left my head. I couldn't remember your name or what I wanted to say. I was lucky to remember who I was. I ran."

He shook his head. "No. Never! I wouldn't forget you, Elizabeth. I couldn't. It was someone else."

She laughed and shook her head. "It was you. It was."

"Then I was blind and deaf and uncaring."

"No. You were famous and I was nothing."

"Don't say that! You are a special person and you always have been and always will be."

She smiled into his eyes and he smiled back a heart-stopping smile. She wanted to lift her lips to meet his, but she caught herself in time. "Thank you for taking my mind off Jill and the baby and Ben."

"For you, anything." His voice was low and tender and the words curled around her heart.

Just then the door burst open and Ben rushed toward them, his face glowing, his red hair wild.

Elizabeth jumped up, gripping Badden's hand. "What, Ben? What?"

"A boy! I have a boy! We have a boy and he has red hair!" Ben clamped his hands on her face and kissed her noisily, then pumped Badden's hand up and down. "A boy! I want to call her parents and mine and the whole world!"

"You're a lucky man, Ben," said Badden huskily. "I'm glad I was here on such a grand occasion."

"You both look very tired," said Ben, really looking at them. "You've been here for hours." He kissed Elizabeth again. "Be a good little sister and go home and get some sleep."

"I will after we see the baby."

"He'll be in the nursery. Just look for the best-looking boy." Ben grinned, then hurried to the pay phone down the hall.

Badden slipped his arm around Elizabeth's waist. "Shall we look at the prize?"

She laughed and nodded, then walked with him down another corridor to the wide glass window where the babies slept in their little plastic beds.

"Oh, Badden," she whispered in awe as she looked at the tiny bundle in the crib marked "Johnson." He lay on his stomach with his red hair uncovered and his tiny fists clenched on the mattress on either side of his head. His eyes were tightly closed and his face looked almost as red as his hair. "He's beautiful."

Badden cleared his throat. "I have never seen a newborn."

"Me neither."

He slipped both arms around her waist and pulled her back against his long, lean frame and they stood there looking at the newborn as if he were a priceless painting.

"I will never forget this day," whispered Badden.

She closed her eyes and leaned her head back. "And neither will I."

NINE
The time for love

The grandfather clock bonged three times as Elizabeth
walked beside Badden up the stairs. She wanted to sleep
for a week, but she didn't want to leave Badden. She
stopped outside her bedroom door and he stopped
beside her.

"Sleep well, Elizabeth," he whispered tenderly.
"You've had quite a day."

"Thank you for being here." She wanted to reach up
and kiss him.

He pushed her hair back and trailed a long finger
down her cheek. She saw his expression change and a
muscle twitched in his cheek. "Since your cowboy
couldn't be here to help you, it's the least I could do.
You've done a lot for me."

She frowned. "Tonight was done as a favor to me?
Just . . . a favor?" she thought. Her stomach tightened
painfully and hot tears stung her eyes.

He looked down. "Good night, Elizabeth. Sleep well."
He opened her door and urged her inside, clicking on
her light. "Good night." He strode to the guest room

and she heard the door open, then close. She stood very still a long time, her head down, her shoulders drooping. She had thought for a while tonight that he loved her. She flushed and slowly closed the door. She'd almost told him that she loved him, that he was her life and that she wanted to be his wife.

She pressed her hands to her burning cheeks. What if she'd said that to him? Oh, it was too terrible to think about!

Finally she slipped between the clean sheets of her bed and closed her eyes. Silently she thanked the Lord for Jill's safe delivery of her son.

As she sank into sleep Badden's image filled her mind and she could feel his heart beating against her. "Oh, Badden," she whispered into her pillow.

Late the next morning she walked downstairs to the kitchen for a glass of orange juice. The house seemed very quiet and for some strange reason fear pricked her skin.

She sipped her orange juice as she walked to the family room, then stopped in the doorway as she saw Toby and Vickie locked in each other's arms. Before she could move Toby looked up and saw her. He flushed with a grin.

"Don't mind us, Elizabeth," he said.

Vickie turned but he wouldn't release her completely. "Did you see Badden yet to say good-bye?"

Elizabeth almost dropped her glass. She swallowed hard. "Is he leaving?" Her voice broke.

Toby nodded. "I helped him load his car awhile ago. He said he'd wait until you woke up before he left."

"Where is he now?"

"Outdoors," said Vickie, reaching for the glass of juice

before it fell from Elizabeth's lifeless fingers.

"Mom and the kids are with him," said Toby with a strange look on his face. "Are you all right, Elizabeth?"

She hurried to the back door, her heart in her mouth. How could he leave? There was a month of summer left. He had to stay. He had to give her that time! What would she do if he left? She might never see him again.

Badden pushed himself up from the picnic table, excused himself, and walked toward her. He looked tall and thin and absolutely beautiful. "Did you sleep well?"

She stopped, her fists doubled at her sides, her pointed chin high. "You can't leave! You have August yet."

"Can we walk?"

She glanced at Vera, Peggy, and Alan, and then back at Badden. "Yes, we'll take a walk. And we'll talk." She wanted to strike out at him.

"Elizabeth," called Vera. "Ben called a few minutes ago to say that Jill and the baby had a good night. He said Jill wants to see you later."

"All right, Mom. I'll go this afternoon." If she had any life left after Badden drove away.

Badden took her arm but she shook his hand off, then walked beside him past the chicken house and up the hill where the family had gone sledding for many winters.

She walked quickly, glad that she'd slipped on sneakers instead of sandals. Finally she stopped in the shade of several oaks. She glared at Badden, her fists on her narrow hips.

"Why are you leaving?"

He stabbed his fingers through his blond hair and groaned. "Don't make it hard, Elizabeth."

She stamped her foot. "Why are you leaving?"

"I am well. I have all my energy back just as you and Marv said. I am ready to get back to work. I called Marv this morning and he said that he had a tour ready for me."

Her chest rose and fell. "When will I see you again?"

He looked down at the ground, then at her. "Maybe never."

"Why?" she cried, tears stinging her hazel eyes.

"You have your cowboy. You don't need me around."

"What cowboy? You mentioned a cowboy last night. Who are you talking about?" she asked angrily.

"Mark McCall. I heard you tell him that you love him. I saw you kiss him." Badden pushed his hands into his dark blue pants and hunched his wide shoulders. "Good-bye, Elizabeth. I've enjoyed knowing you and your family. You're all special people."

She shook her head dumbly. "You're wrong, Badden. Mark is a friend, nothing more. I have no cowboy." What was she doing? If she kept on she'd be throwing herself at his feet, begging him to stay, to love her. She turned toward the house. "I am glad I have my career, and I'm glad that you're going to continue with yours."

She took three steps and he said softly, "Elizabeth."

She stopped, her head down, her hair swinging forward to cover her flushed cheeks.

Cricket barked in the distance and a grasshopper hopped across Elizabeth's foot.

"Elizabeth, thank you for teaching me to swim."

She nodded, but couldn't turn.

"And to ride."

Hot tears slipped from her eyes and down her face.

"And to live." His hand closed around her arm and he turned her to him, gently lifting her face. "You're crying."

"No, I'm not," she whispered hoarsely as she wiped

away her tears. He was quiet so long that she finally looked up. His piercing gaze unnerved her and she stepped back. "Why are you looking at me like that?"

"I am trying to see into your heart."

She quickly lowered her eyes. "It would make you laugh." She heard him step closer and she smelled his after-shave lotion and she wanted to turn and run before he learned the truth.

"Why do you suddenly look afraid, Elizabeth? Why can't you let me see what you're thinking and feeling? You have seen my heart, and you know how I feel."

Her eyes widened in surprise. "When have I seen your heart? When have I seen how you feel?"

He gripped her arms painfully, and his eyes darkened with passion. "You've given me life. You're in my mind every waking moment. You're in my dreams at night. I have kissed you and held you and talked to you about myself. The wall that I built so carefully to keep everyone out is down, taken down by you bit by bit. And then you dare to say that you have not seen my heart!"

He hauled her to him and his mouth closed over hers. She locked her fingers behind his head as she returned his kiss with equal fervor and his words continued to ring through her head and her heart.

He loved her!

He buried his face in her hair. "I love you, Elizabeth Johnson. I love you more than life itself."

"Then why are you leaving?"

He looked down into her upturned face. "I don't want pity, nor hero worship, nor friendship."

"But you are my hero! You're my best friend!" She

showered kisses on his face but he pushed her away. Her face fell and she stared helplessly at him. "I love you."

He rubbed his hand across his eyes. "As you love other friends?" She started to speak, but he raised his hand to silence her. "I need more than your friendship. I need you every minute of every day. I need you for the rest of my life."

She flung her arms wide and laughed with her head back. "Oh, Badden Lindsay! If you asked me, I would give up my piano. If you asked me, I'd stay home and cook your meals and rub your neck when it aches from hours of practice. If you asked me."

He stared at her, then finally read the message of love in her eyes. He reached for her and she willingly stepped into his arms to be pulled close to his heart. His lips met hers and she kissed him with the same passion that she felt in his kiss.

After a long time he said, "When will you marry me?"

"Tomorrow," she whispered, her eyes shining happily.

He kissed her again, then held her away, his face very serious. "I would never ask you to give up your career. It is as much a part of you as your beautiful eyes and your kind nature."

She laughed happily as she touched his dear face. "I will continue my career as long as it doesn't interfere with our life together."

He shrugged. "We have Marv Secord to set up our tours. We'll tell him to book us together. We'll become a team."

She nodded. "I like that. Badden and Elizabeth Lindsay. It sounds wonderful!" She tugged on his hand. "Let's go tell my family. They'll be glad to hear that they're going to have a wedding in the family again."

"Wait." He smiled tenderly as he pulled her close again. "I want you to myself just a little longer. I love your family, but there are so many of them!"

On August twenty-eighth Elizabeth stood in the back room of the church dressed in a long white gown made of satin with lace at the cuffs of the long sleeves, around the high neck, and in scallops at the hem. She smiled shakily at Vera. "Do I look all right, Mom?"

"You look beautiful. Bend down a little and let me fix the veil." Vera finally stepped back with a satisfied smile. She was dressed in a pale blue dress with a scoop neck and short sleeves. She blinked away tears. "Our little Libby is grown up and getting married."

"I look very different from that skinny, ragged, foul-mouthed girl who walked into your home thirteen years ago." She touched Vera's soft cheek. "Thank you for loving me and for being my mother."

"You are very welcome. You are very precious to me. I'm thankful that the man you chose is so perfect for you."

"He is pretty nice, isn't he?" She grinned and Vera laughed.

The door opened and Susan and Jill walked in. They were dressed in flowered dresses with yellow and green tones and carried white and yellow daisies.

"Tammy will be here in a minute," said Susan as she pushed a stray hair into place. "Oh, Elizabeth, you look gorgeous!"

"You do!" agreed Jill, her eyes filling with tears.

Elizabeth hugged her, then Vera had to adjust her veil all over again.

"Kevin called just before we left the house," said Vera

to Susan and Jill. "He said he's bringing his future wife for us to meet."

Susan exclaimed in delight while Elizabeth thought of the little blond boy who had always been overweight and worn glasses. Now he was as tall as Chuck, not overweight, and wore contacts. And he was going to get married. That left Toby. If Vickie stayed a little longer, then Toby might be having a wedding, too.

The Johnson family was growing bigger and bigger.

Chuck stuck his head in and grinned. "Is the father of the bride allowed a little time with his girl?"

"Come in, Dad," said Elizabeth, catching his hand and tugging him into the small room.

"We'll see you at the altar," said Susan, kissing Elizabeth's flushed cheek. "You're my own special sister and I love you."

Jill clasped Elizabeth's hand. "Ben and Matthew and I love you and want the very best for you."

"Thank you, Jill."

Vera kissed Elizabeth's cheek. "Be happy, darling."

"I will, Mom." Elizabeth stood beside Chuck as the others walked out, closing the door. She turned to Chuck and hugged him. He was only a couple of inches taller and looked very handsome in his light suit and white shirt. "I love you, Dad. You are the very best dad in the world."

"I love you, Elizabeth Johnson. You came into my home and my heart. I'll never forget the day I drove in the driveway in my pickup and you were standing there with your battered suitcase, trying to get to town. I wanted to gather you in my arms and protect you from all the pain in the world. No little girl should've had the hurt and the unkind treatment that you'd received all your life. I wanted to blank out those bad years and fill your life with love and happiness."

"You did, Dad."

"With God's help."

"Yes." She rubbed the back of Chuck's hand where little red hairs grew. "Badden and I have agreed together to continue to study God's Word and grow more and more like Jesus. We want to share the love and happiness that we've found with others."

"You are marrying a fine young man, Elizabeth. You'll have a loving husband and a successful career."

"The little aid kid who had nothing now has everything." She blinked back tears and kissed Chuck's cheek. "Thanks, Dad."

Chuck picked up her bouquet and studied it, then looked at her. "I talked to Marie Dobbs this morning."

Elizabeth stiffened.

"She said she wouldn't come and ruin your day, but that she will be thinking of you. She said she hopes you have a happy marriage and a happy life. I told her you would."

"Thanks." Her heart went out to her mother who had never had any happiness, and who wouldn't until she accepted Christ as her Lord and Savior.

"Honey, I'm glad all your anger and fear and bitterness toward Marie Dobbs are gone. Continue to pray for her, and I will, too."

Nolen poked his head in the door and whispered. "It's time, Elizabeth. Oh, you look beautiful!"

"Thank you." Her face glowed as she adjusted her veil and took Chuck's arm. "This is it, Dad."

"I love you, my precious Elizabeth."

"I love you, Dad. No matter where I go, I will think of you and the Johnson farm."

"You and Badden will always have a room waiting for you."

Elizabeth nodded, then walked to the aisle and stood with her hand on Chuck's arm until Susan, Jill, and Tammy were in place along with Ben, Kevin, and Toby. Pastor Zimmer faced the audience and Badden stood waiting. As if he felt her presence, he turned and she smiled down the long aisle at him. He smiled and the music swelled and she began her long walk toward her new life.

She devoured Badden with her eyes and he returned the look with an intensity that sent her pulse racing.

Finally when Chuck handed her over to Badden she was able to touch him and he gripped her arm as if he'd never let her go.

He spoke his vows and she spoke hers and she knew their marriage would last a lifetime. He slipped a ring on her finger and she in turn placed one on his finger.

Pastor Zimmer spoke a few words, then prayed over them. "You may kiss the bride," he said to Badden.

Badden looked at her and she stood very still as he slowly lifted the veil and draped it over her head. He smiled and she smiled, then he slid his arms around her and she slipped her arms around him. He kissed her, their first kiss as husband and wife. Their eyes met and they turned together to face the church full of people.

"Friends and family, I want to present Mr. and Mrs. Badden Lindsay," said Pastor Zimmer proudly.

The music swelled and Elizabeth smiled, then they rushed arm in arm down the aisle. The time for love had come.